D0236117

lauren child

whoops! But it wasn't me

PUFFIN

Text based on script written by
Bridget Hurst and Carol Noble

Illustrations from the TV animation

produced by Tiger Aspect

PUFFIN BOOKS
Published by the Penguin Group: London, New York, Ireland, Australia,
Canada, India, New Zealand and South Africa
Penguin Books Ltd, Registered Offices: 80 Strand, London WC2R 0RL, England

www.penguin.com

First published 2006
1 3 5 7 9 10 8 6 4 2
Text and illustrations copyright © Lauren Child/Tiger Aspect Productions Limited, 2006
The Charlie and Lola logo is a trademark of Lauren Child
All rights reserved
The moral right of the author/illustrator has been asserted
Made and printed in China
ISBN-13: 978-0-141-38241-8
ISBN-10: 0-141-38241-4

I have this little sister Lola.
She is small and very funny.
Sometimes Lola likes to play
with my things.
Usually I don't mind.

One day I come home from school
with the best thing I have ever made.

Lola says, "Ooooh!"

I say,
"It took me **ten** days,
     three hours and **forty** minutes
to make the outside,
      which is called
the **superstructure**...

"... It's built from

three

cereal

packets,

ten
yoghurt
pots,

28 bottle tops,

157 sweet wrappers and a roll of extra-wide tinfoil...

two whole tubes of glue,
three pots of paint
and half a roll of sticky tape."

Lola says, "Ooooh!"

I say, "Don't touch it!
This rocket is really breakable.
I don't mind you playing with
most of my things,
but you must double,
triple promise me
you will NEVER play
with this."

"Let's **play** something
        else then," says Lola.
    I say, "I've got to see Marv."
"But what am I going to do?" says Lola.
        And I say, "Why don't you **play**
    with Soren Lorensen?"

Soren Lorensen is Lola's imaginary friend.
No one can see him except for Lola.

And Lola says,
    "Yes. Soren Lorensen **always** wants
to **play** with me."

"Hello, Soren Lorensen," says Lola.
"Charlie's gone to see Marv, so we can play
a very good game, can't we?"

And Soren Lorensen says,
     "Yes, with those two laughing
hyenas that are brothers and twins."

Lola says, "Yes, and Ellie,
     the tiny, small elephant.

"Where will the adventure be?"

Soren Lorensen says,
"In the place where all the **animals** live."

And Lola says,
"In a place a long way away."

"Oh no," says Soren Lorensen. "Ellie is really **sad** because he doesn't like the hyenas laughing at him and he's very far from home."

"Those **hyena** brother twins are **meanies**,
aren't they?" says Lola.
"What are we going to do?"

"We can't leave Ellie all sad," says Lola.
"He must go back to his nice friends in elephant land...
but how are we going to get him there?"

Then Soren Lorensen points to the rocket.

Lola says,
"But that is an extremely breakable and special rocket
and Charlie said that we should NOT ever
NEVER touch it or play with it."

"That's true," says Soren Lorensen, "but I think
what Charlie meant was that if we did play
with it, we must be extra specially
careful and not break it."

So Lola reaches up to get the rocket.

Soren Lorensen says,
    "Remember to be extra
specially careful, Lola."

And Lola says,

"I am!
I am being
extra specially
careful!"

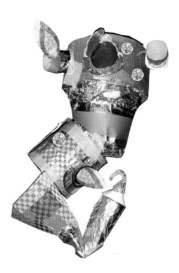

Then she says,

"Whoops!"

Lola looks at the
pieces of broken rocket.
"You know, I think that
when things are **broken**
they can **always** be
mended together and made like **new**..."

"If we both act **normally**, Lola,
then Charlie will **never know**
we did it," says Soren Lorensen.

Lola whispers,

"No, he'll **never know.**"

When I get home I shout,
"My rocket!
Lola!
Did you break
my rocket?"

Lola says,
"I didn't break your rocket, Charlie.
You absolutely told me to NOT
ever NEVER touch it... ever."

I say,
"You are telling a big lie, Lola!
And you know it!"

"Don't tell Mum!"
says Lola. "Wait, Charlie!
I just have to quickly talk
to Soren Lorensen."

Lola says, "Do you think we should tell Charlie
what really happened?"
Soren Lorensen says, "Maybe we should tell him
that somebody else broke the rocket?"
And Lola says, "Oh yes! Because it is nearly true!"

So Lola comes to talk to me.
"Charlie, Soren Lorensen and me have got something
very **extremely** important to tell you."

I say, "What?"

Lola says,
"It is the real **true** story of who **broke**
your special **rocket**.

"Well, me and Soren Lorensen were **playing** in our room, Charlie, and Ellie needed to go in your **rocket**.

And I didn't think that was a good idea, but Ellie wouldn't listen.

So we all squeezed
into the rocket
so that we could
go and find
all Ellie's
nice friends.

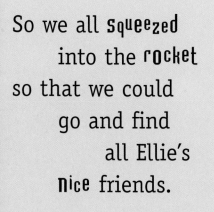

It was a real squish. But we did it.

"We took off. Higher and higher, right round the whole world. And then we went down and down,

and

down

and

down

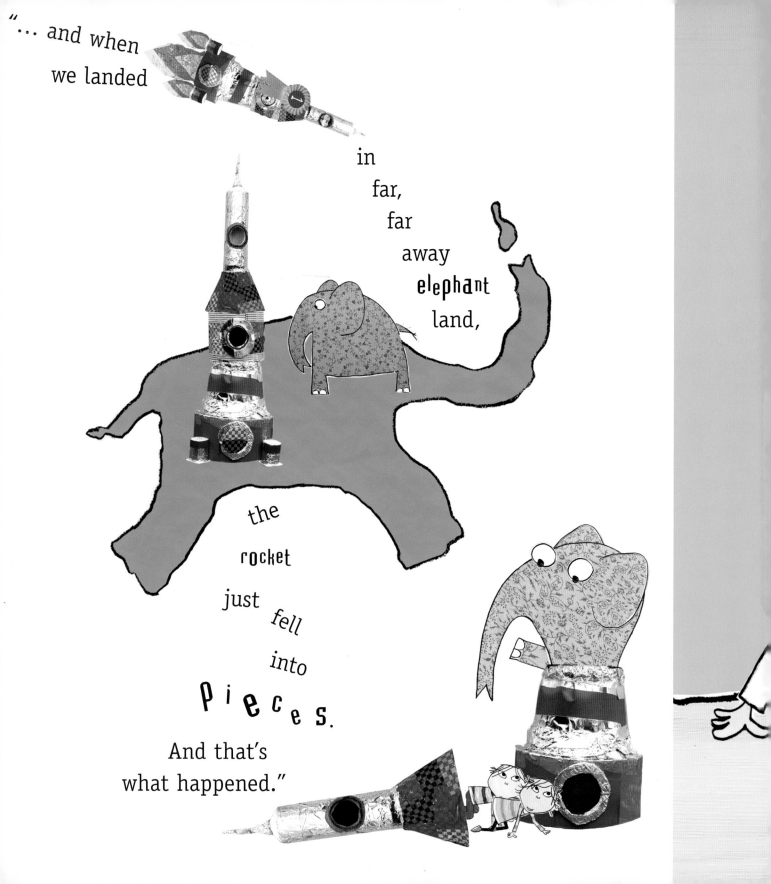

"... and when
we landed

in
far,
far
away elephant
land,

the
rocket
just fell
into
Pieces.
And that's
what happened."

I say,
"Right.
I'm going
to tell
Mum."

"Oh dear, I don't think he
believed us," says Soren Lorensen.

Lola says,
"I think I have to tell
Charlie the **truth**. But will it
make Charlie **like** me again?"

Soren Lorensen says,
"Yes, as long as you
say **sorry** too."

Lola knocks at the door.
"Soren Lorensen
really wants to say **sorry**
for breaking your
rocket, Charlie."

So I just shut
the door.

Then there's another knock
and Lola says,
"It was me that broke
your rocket. I was playing
with Ellie and just as I was
getting your extremely
special rocket down from
the really high shelf...
it fell and broke
into lots
of pieces.

I am really
ever so very sorry
for breaking your
extremely special rocket,
Charlie."

And I say,
"Are you **really**, Lola?"

Lola says, "Really, **really**
truly **sorry**."
And she does look really very sorry.
So I say,
"That's OK. At least you've
told the **truth**."

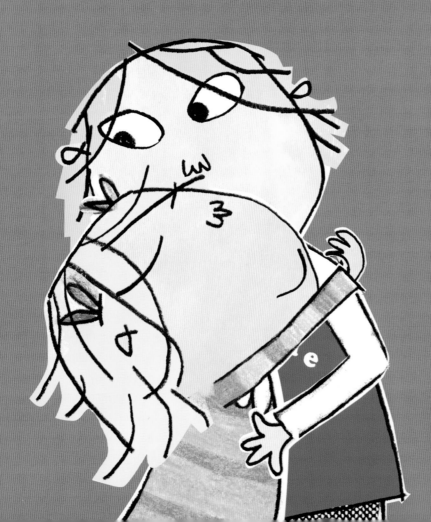

Then Lola sees the rocket.

"You **mended** it, Charlie!" she says.

And I say,
"Yes, Lola, I've **mended** it."

"I like it," says Lola.
I say,
"Don't touch it!"